Just
Like
Daddy

Just Like Daddy

© 2015 Ovi Nedelcu

Published in the United States and Canada by POW!
a division of powerHouse Packaging & Supply, Inc.

ISBN: 978-1-57687-756-2
Library of Congress Control Number: 2014948085

powerHouse Packaging & Supply, Inc.
37 Main Street, Brooklyn, NY 11201-1021
info@POWkidsbooks.com
www.POWkidsbooks.com
www.powerHouseBooks.com
www.powerHousePackaging.com

First edition, 2015

10 9 8 7 6 5 4 3 2 1

Printed in China

Just Like Daddy

OVI NEDELCU

Brooklyn, NY

Morning is my **favorite time!**

When I wake up I'm **rested** and **excited** to see the sunrise!

Just
like
Daddy.

I get dressed in my **super outfit,** ready to **take** on the **day!**

Just
like
Daddy.

But before I head out
on my adventures,
I make sure I eat a big, healthy
breakfast.

Just
like
Daddy.

HEALTHY
CRISPS!

MADE WITH
ORGANIC
TREE BARK!

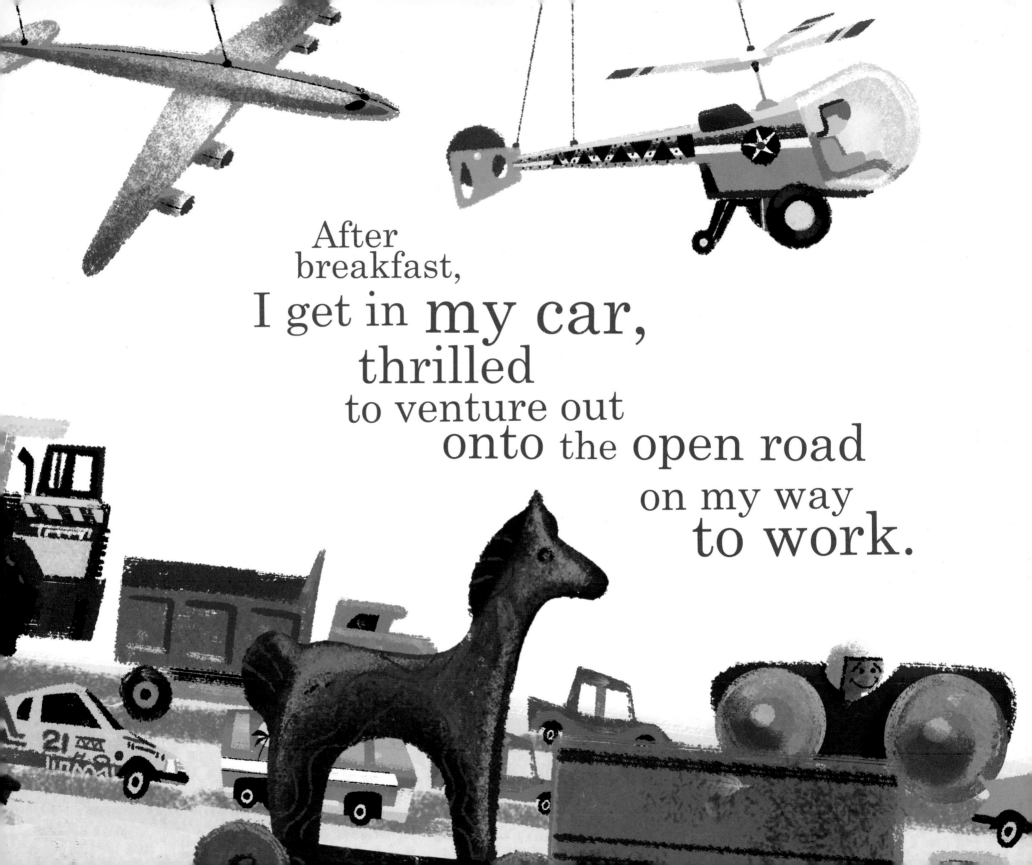

After breakfast, I get in my car, thrilled to venture out onto the open road on my way to work.

Just
like
Daddy.

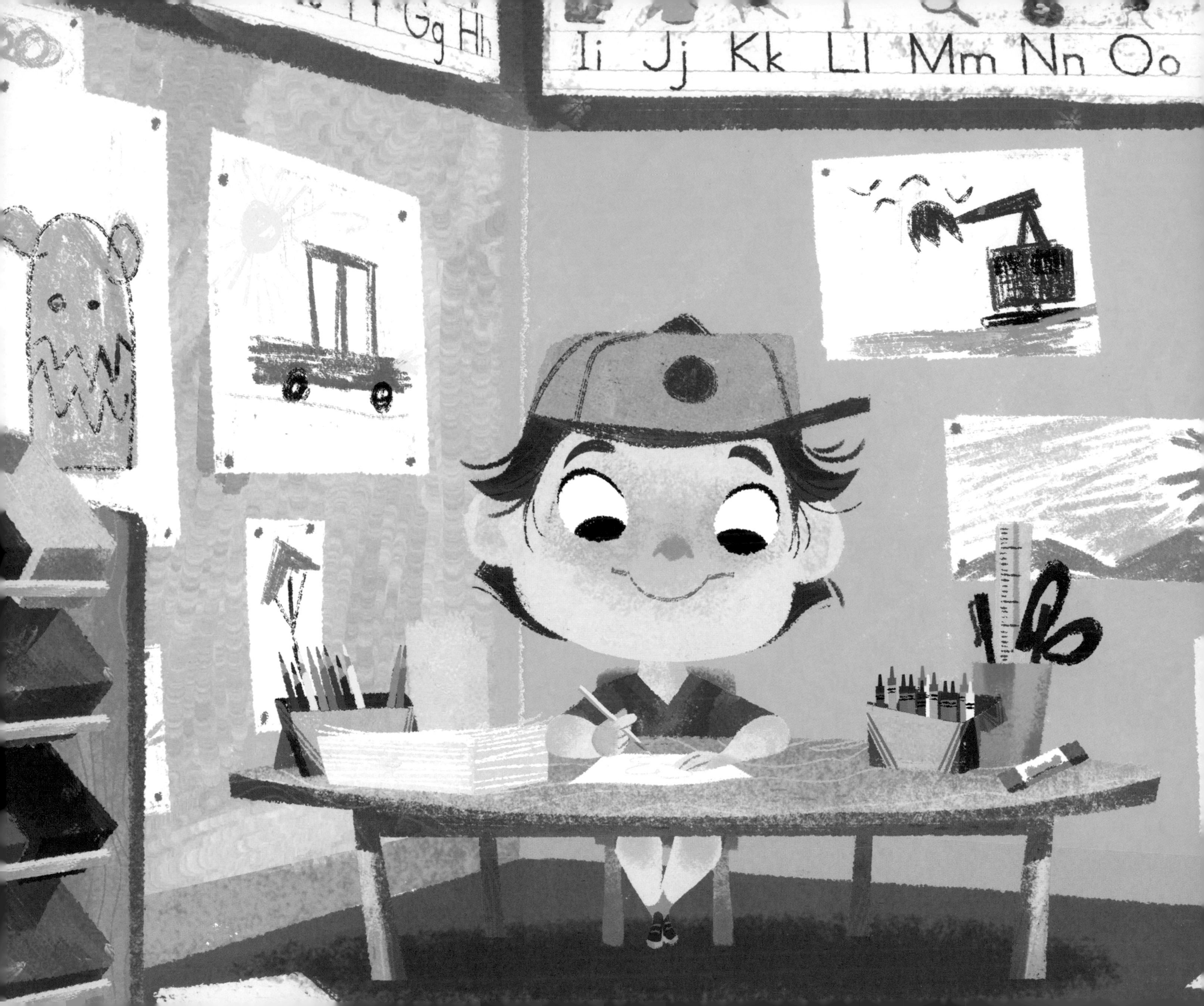
Gg Hh
Ii Jj Kk Ll Mm Nn Oo

Once I get to work, I have so much fun doing all of my projects.

Just
like
Daddy.

After dinner, I like to open my books and have a few good bedtime stories to take my mind off a hard day's work.

PEET

Just
like
Daddy.

TAXES

PHONE
BILL

FEE

JURY
DUTY

ENDLESS
FEES

VOTE FOR
ME

And when we go to bed,
we dream about the weekend.

Together.

To my family.